roar!

But Lion is busy **roaring** as loud
as he can, so he can't hear.

"Parrot, Parrot, can I ask you a question?" squeaks Little Mouse.

But Parrot is busy **squawking**

up in the tree, so he can't hear.

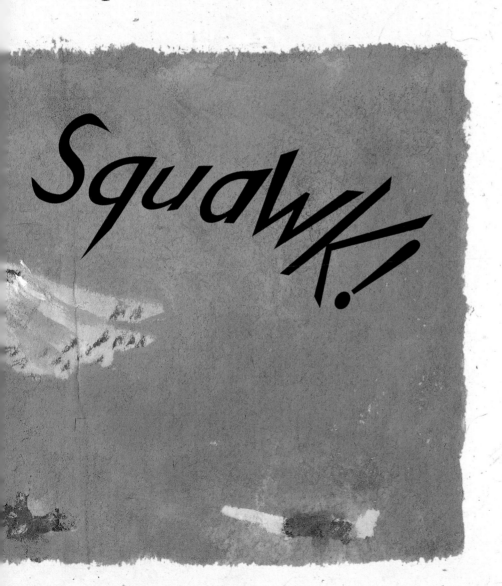

Squawk!

"Crocodile, Crocodile, can I ask you a question?" squeaks Little Mouse.

But Crocodile is busy **snapping** her
enormous jaws, so she can't hear.

snap!

Munch!

"Panda, Panda, can I ask you a question?"
squeaks Little Mouse, from a branch.

But Panda is busy **munching** her breakfast bamboo, so she can't hear.

"Turtle, Turtle, can I ask you a
question?" squeaks Little Mouse.

Splash!

But Turtle is busy **splashing**

in the water, so she can't hear.

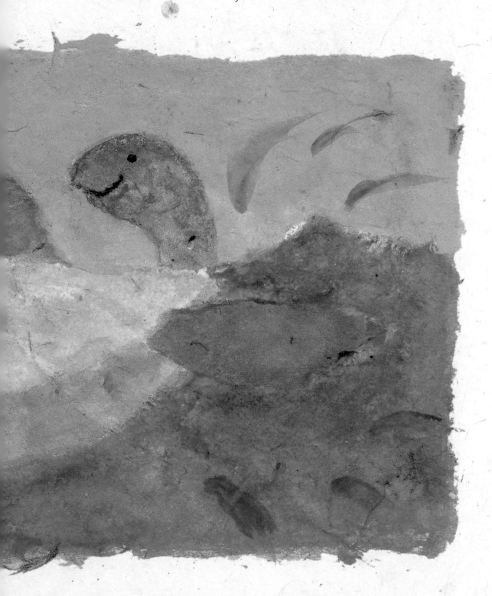

"Little Mice, Little Mice, can I ask you all a question?" squeaks Little Mouse.

squeak!

squeak!

squeak!

squeak!

squeak!

squeak!

The Little Mice

stop squeaking.

Yes!

Can you remember the names of these animal friends?

Lion

The Asiatic lion can now roam safely in the huge Gir National Park and Lion Sanctuary in India.

Parrot

The New Zealand government started the fight to save the flightless kakapo parrot from extinction in the 1950's.